1853

MEET
Cécile
An American Girl

By DENISE LEWIS PATRICK

ILLUSTRATIONS CHRISTINE KORNACKI

VIGNETTES CINDY SALANS ROSENHEIM

★ American Girl®

The American Girls

1764

Kaya, an adventurous Nez Perce girl whose deep love for horses and respect for nature nourish her spirit

1774

Felicity, a spunky, spritely colonial girl, full of energy and independence

1824

Josefina, a Hispanic girl whose heart and hopes are as big as the New Mexico sky

1853

Cécile and Marie-Grace, two girls whose friendship helps them—and New Orleans— survive terrible times

1854

Kirsten, a pioneer girl of strength and spirit who settles on the frontier

1864  ADDY, a courageous girl determined to be free in the midst of the Civil War

1904  SAMANTHA, a bright Victorian beauty, an orphan raised by her wealthy grandmother

1914  REBECCA, a lively girl with dramatic flair growing up in New York City

1934  KIT, a clever, resourceful girl facing the Great Depression with spirit and determination

1944  MOLLY, who schemes and dreams on the home front during World War Two

1974  JULIE, a fun-loving girl from San Francisco who faces big changes—and creates a few of her own

11-9-7
BfT 695

Published by American Girl Publishing, Inc.
Copyright © 2011 by American Girl, LLC

Questions or comments? Call 1-800-845-0005, visit **americangirl.com**, or write to Customer Service, American Girl, 8400 Fairway Place, Middleton, WI 53562-0497.

Printed in China
11 12 13 14 15 16 LEO 10 9 8 7 6 5 4 3 2 1

All American Girl marks, Cécile™, Cécile Rey™, Marie-Grace™, and Marie-Grace Gardner™ are trademarks of American Girl, LLC.

Profound appreciation to Mary Niall Mitchell, Associate Professor of History, University of New Orleans; Sally Kittredge Reeves, former Notarial Archivist, New Orleans; and Thomas A. Klingler, Associate Professor, Department of French and Italian, Tulane University

PICTURE CREDITS

The following individuals and organizations have generously given permission to reprint images contained in "Looking Back": p. 89—portrait of Maritcha Lyons, Photographs and Prints Division, Schomburg Center for Research in Black Culture, The New York Public Library, Astor, Lenox and Tilden Foundations; pp. 90–91—Royal Street scene by Boyd Cruise, courtesy of Michelle Favrot Heidelberg; Wisconsin Historical Society, image WHi-72895 (fan); *Portrait of Marie Lassus of New Orleans* by Jean-Philippe Potteau, New Orleans Museum of Art: Museum purchase, Clarence John Laughlin Photographic Society Fund 86.113; pp. 92–93—Collection of Jack & Ann Brittain and children, photo by Don Sepulvado (portrait); courtesy of the John Carter Brown Library at Brown University (Haiti scene detail); Louisiana Division/City Archives, New Orleans Public Library (William Carret document); pp. 94–95—© James R. Lockhart (Creole-style cottages); sculpture, courtesy of the Collections of Louisiana State Museum; © Alison Wright/Corbis (cemetery); pp. 96–97—*French Opera House* by Boyd Cruise (detail), collection of Mr. Joseph H. Epstein, Jr.; The Historic New Orleans Collection, accession no. 1985.212 (woman in tignon); *Three Sisters of the Copeland Family, 1854,* by William Matthew Prior, 1806–1873, oil on canvas, 68.26 x 92.71 cm (26⅞ x 36½ in.), Museum of Fine Arts, Boston, Bequest of Martha C. Karolik for the M. and M. Karolik Collection of American Paintings, 1815–1865, 48.467, photograph © 2011 Museum of Fine Arts, Boston.

Photo of the author by Fran Baltzer

Cataloging-in-Publication Data available from the Library of Congress

THE HEART OF THIS STORY
IS DEDICATED TO MY GRANDMOTHER,
LILLIAN MILTON LEWIS
OF NEW ORLEANS

Cécile and her family speak both English and French, just as many people from New Orleans did. You'll see some French words in this book. For help in pronouncing or understanding the foreign words, look in the glossary on page 98.

TABLE OF CONTENTS

CÉCILE'S FAMILY AND FRIENDS

CHAPTER ONE
KINGS AND CHOCOLATE   1

CHAPTER TWO
FREE PEOPLE OF COLOR   19

CHAPTER THREE
A NEW FRIEND AND GOOD NEWS   29

CHAPTER FOUR
MARDI GRAS SEASON   40

CHAPTER FIVE
DANCING FAIRIES . 57

CHAPTER SIX
SECRETS AND PROMISES   73

LOOKING BACK   89

GLOSSARY OF FRENCH WORDS   98

A SNEAK PEEK AT
MARIE-GRACE AND THE ORPHANS   103

CÉCILE'S FAMILY

PAPA
*Cécile's father, a
warm, gentle man
and a successful
sculptor*

MAMAN
*Cécile's mother, who is
firm but kind and is a
good businesswoman*

CÉCILE
*A confident, curious
nine-year-old girl who
loves the limelight*

ARMAND
*Cécile's older brother,
who has been studying
in Paris, France*

GRAND-PÈRE
*Cécile's loving
grandfather, a retired sailor
with many tales to tell*

TANTE OCTAVIA
AND RENÉ
*Maman's widowed sister
and her son, who live
with Cécile's family*

MADEMOISELLE
OCÉANE
*A French opera singer
who gives voice lessons*

MARIE-GRACE
GARDNER
*A girl who has just
moved back to
New Orleans after
several years away*

MATHILDE
*The Reys' housekeeper
and cook*

ELLEN
The Reys' housemaid

KINGS AND
CHOCOLATE

January 1853

Cécile Rey breathed in the spicy scent of the almost-bare Christmas tree. She looked closely at the delicate ball of blue glass in her hands. She turned the ornament slowly in the morning sunlight and imagined that the parlor and everything in it were floating in a pale blue sky.

"Maman," she asked, "why do we spend so much time hanging pretty things *on* the tree, if we only have to take them off again?"

Maman looked up from the box that she was lining with soft cloth. "Because they are *de fête*—festive, cheerful," she replied, switching from perfect

1

English to French and back again.

"Queen Victoria of England has a Christmas tree," said Maman's sister, Tante Octavia. She peeked through the thick branches as she removed another ornament.

"That's true. It's here in the *Picayune*." Cécile's grandfather nodded from his armchair and rustled the newspaper. "And don't forget, our last name is Rey," Grand-père added. "That means 'king,' you know."

"But I'm Cécile of New Orleans, not a king— not even a queen!" Cécile shook her curls. Christmas trees were a new fashion, and even though they were pretty, Cécile thought they were too much work.

"*AAAWWWK,*" a croaking voice squawked from a darkened corner. "*Not even a queen! Not even a queen!*" Cécile's pet parrot ruffled his brilliant blue and green feathers and cackled from his tall perch near the window.

"Hush, Cochon," Cécile said, stuffing her hand into her apron pocket. "Presents for you." Cochon fell silent when he saw the pecans in Cécile's open palm. She dropped the nuts on a small table and watched him glide over to peck at them greedily. What a perfect name he had—it meant "pig" in French.

Mathilde, the housekeeper and cook, laughed. "I'll bet you liked *your* presents well enough, too, Miss Cécé," she said, neatly stacking boxes.

Cécile smiled and carefully wrapped the glass ball in a square of old cloth. "It's true," she agreed in a soft voice. "I love Christmas and New Year's Day—and not only because of the presents."

"And why else?" Grand-père asked over the top of his paper.

"On Christmas Eve, we go to Midnight Mass at the beautiful cathedral," Cécile said, "and I get to stay up very late eating gumbo and listening to your wonderful stories, Grand-père!"

The grown-ups laughed, recalling Grand-père's tales of his Christmases in faraway places when he was a young sailor.

"And then, on Christmas Day," Cécile went on dreamily, "I *love* when we play charades." She smiled. She was better than anyone at acting out words in that game. Only her brother, Armand, could sometimes do as well.

"Everything would have been just perfect if only

Armand were here, too," she added wistfully. Her older brother was studying in Paris, France. He had been away for two long years.

"He'll return this August to work with your father," Grand-père reminded her.

"But August is a lifetime away, Grand-père!" Cécile thought of the many months until Armand's return. Was Armand, so far away in Paris, wishing right now that time would pass faster, too?

She sighed. Now that the holidays were over, Cécile realized, it was back to boring lessons with Monsieur Lejeune, her tutor. If only he would allow her to recite more and do less grammar! Maybe her voice teacher, Mademoiselle Océane, would let her recite a poem to music, she thought. Cécile was much better at reciting than singing.

"Cheer up." Mathilde patted her on the head. "Mardi Gras season is coming soon!"

Cécile's face brightened. In New Orleans, the weeks between early January and late February or early March made up the Mardi Gras season. Everyone went to parties and concerts and dances— even children. Every year Cécile and all her friends dressed in costume for the biggest dance, the

4

Children's Ball. And every year, Cécile had trouble deciding just what costume to choose. Should she become an elegant ballet dancer? Or a fantastical character from one of the plays she had seen? More than anything, Cécile wanted a costume that would stand out from all the others.

Maman interrupted her thoughts. "Speaking of your brother, have you written to him this week?"

Cécile bit her lip. "No, Maman. Not yet." She had been meaning to sit down and write a letter, she really had. But writing to Armand was hard to do. Somehow, words came easily to her when she was talking, but they just refused to come out on paper. And Armand's letters to her were filled with such funny stories and amusing little sketches of his life in Paris! Compared to his, her letters seemed quite dull. Still, she had to try—she didn't want him to think she'd forgotten him.

Cécile twisted a bit of packing cloth in her hands. Maman looked stern.

"Why don't Cécile and I go out for a bit?" Tante Octavia said quickly. "We'll take the holiday gift baskets to La Maison. Then Cécé will have more to write about." Tante Octavia stood right beside

Maman. Tante had the same long, straight nose and dark almond eyes as Maman. They had the same thick black hair. But Maman's skin was fair, and Tante Octavia's was like Cécile's own—a golden brown.

Maman glanced at her sister. "Well..." Maman began. Cécile stood up hopefully.

"Oh, please, Maman?" Cécile rushed to her mother's side. She did enjoy visiting La Maison, a home for older people of color who had no families to take care of them. She always thought of Grand-père when she went. "And you come with us!"

"Ah, *oui!*" Maman agreed. "Go on then, but without me this time. I've much to do." Maman not only ran the household, she also managed all the houses and other property that she and her sister Octavia had inherited from their parents long ago. She was a very good businesswoman.

Maman kissed the top of Cécile's head. Then she shooed Cécile and Tante Octavia away like kittens. They were both into their cloaks and out the door before Maman could change her mind.

The chilly January air made Cécile's cheeks tingle. She and her aunt walked arm in arm along Dumaine Street, each carrying a tightly covered palmetto basket. Cécile's was full of fruit and sweet rolls. Tante's held handmade shawls. Maman and Tante Octavia had knitted several, and Cécile had proudly crocheted one all by herself.

"You know," Tante Octavia said kindly as they turned onto St. Peter Street, "Armand is probably very glad to get letters from you, Cécé. Why didn't you write to him this week?"

Cécile felt a twinge of guilt. "It's just that . . . well, it's so hard for me to know *what* to write."

"Just remember how much you love him, and the words will come," Tante said gently.

"I'll start as soon as we get home," Cécile promised. She felt lucky to have such an understanding aunt to talk to. She pressed closer to Tante Tay. "I'm very sad that Uncle Henry passed away"—Tante's husband had died six months ago in an accident at the shipyard where he'd worked—"but I'm so glad that you left Philadelphia and came back to live with us here in New Orleans."

"Thank you, *chérie*," Tante Tay said softly, giving Cécile a squeeze.

They had reached the square at the center of the French Quarter, the oldest part of the city. Bright new brick buildings edged the square on two sides. On  another stood the stately white-stuccoed front of the cathedral. Busy shoppers crisscrossed the square, and vendors wandered around it selling everything from dried herbs to teaspoons.

"Oh, look—it's Cécile!" someone called.

Cécile and her aunt turned at the same moment. Two girls were coming along the stone walk behind them.

"Aren't those the girls we chatted with at the theater last week?" Tante asked cheerfully. "You must go and say hello to your friends. We have time."

Cécile wanted to explain that the Metoyer sisters weren't exactly her *friends,* but they were approaching too quickly for her to say anything more.

"Fanny! Agnès!" Cécile stepped forward to meet them. She managed a small smile.

"Hello, Cécile." Fanny tossed her long black curls

and looked down her nose at Cécile with sharp eyes. "Lovely to see you again," she said with pretended politeness. "Didn't you just adore the play last week?"

"Oui—" Cécile began, but Agnès cut in.

"Don't you love Sister's new coat? That style is the rage in Paris!" Agnès chirped. Cécile couldn't help noticing that Fanny's wool coat did look very smart with its double row of shining gold buttons, and its bright blue color set off her light brown skin perfectly.

Agnès gave Cécile a head-to-toe look, her stare lingering on Cécile's bare hands. "But I guess you don't care much about fashion, do you?"

Cécile squeezed the handle of her basket tightly. She'd forgotten her gloves again. *Not ladylike*, Agnès was probably thinking.

"Are you shopping for Mardi Gras?" Fanny inquired. "*We've* had wonderful luck with *our* shopping today." Fanny waved toward a boy standing just behind Agnès. His face was almost hidden by the pile of boxes and parcels he carried. With a start, Cécile realized that he was a slave.

Cécile knew that some families of color in the city owned slaves. But she'd heard Grand-père say many times that no matter how much money he had, he would never own another person.

"We're on our way to do *important* work," Cécile huffed. "We're taking gifts to La Maison."

Agnès frowned. "You're going to the home for old people? But why? After we drop our packages off, we're going to a wonderful tea at Marie Conant's house." She nodded to her sister. "Come, Fanny. We mustn't be late!" She spun on her dainty kid boots and sashayed away, leaving Fanny and the boy hurrying to follow.

Cécile took a deep breath, feeling for a moment as if she'd just stepped out of a tight closet. Then she tossed her head. Though she *did* like to dress up, the parties and teas were really always the same old thing, full of boring gossip and girls showing off their new dresses and fancy manners. She'd much rather go to La Maison. The people there were always happy to see her, and they often asked her to recite poems or act out little stories.

"Oh, Tante Tay," Cécile said brightly as her aunt caught up to her, "I know what I'll do at La Maison today—I'll perform a scene from the play we saw last week!"

She skipped along, happily planning out loud. She had already put the Metoyer sisters completely out of her mind.

In the quiet parlor later that day, Cécile's pen scratched across paper as she worked on her letter to Armand. Nearby, Maman and Tante Tay did needlework, and Cochon dozed on his perch.

Cécile dotted her last *i* and held her paper up to catch the fading afternoon light. It would have been easier to see if she'd started earlier in the day, the way Maman had wanted. But, she realized with a smile, Armand wouldn't mind messy handwriting.

Dear Armand,

Do you miss me as much as I miss you? I hope you had a wonderful Christmas in Paris. Is it snowing there? I wish I could see snow! All we have in New Orleans is rain, rain, rain. At least the Mardi Gras parties start soon. I don't know what costume to wear to the Children's Ball. I wish you were here to help me decide. You always have the best ideas!

Here is some news—I was the star of a play today! Well, it was only one scene, and there was no stage or costumes, but no matter. I acted out a scene from a play for all my friends at La Maison. I managed to play three characters and make them all quite different. Everyone laughed at the funny parts and applauded when I was done. They said I was very good. I'll perform the scene for you when you come home—I hope you'll like it, too.

Well, I must go now. Everything else is very boring. Besides, Maman complains when I use too much of her ink—and then she also complains when I don't write! So what am I to do? Anyway, everyone sends love. I'm counting the days until you come home—

Your loving sister,

Cécé

Cécile slipped her letter into a stiff envelope. Then she pressed a little wax flower onto the flap to seal it tight. Would Armand open her letter the minute it arrived, as she did his?

"Very good, Cécile," Maman said from across the parlor. "Now, *ma petite,* about Mardi Gras. Why not be a princess for the ball?" Maman's knitting needles clicked as she spoke.

"Oh, Maman, not a princess again!" Cécile turned and her little cousin, René, squealed and ran to her, tipping the basket of yarn that his mother was using for her needlework. Cécile quickly got down onto her knees to collect the tumbling balls of yarn.

Tante Octavia stopped her needlepoint to watch Cécile scoop up a handful of pink wool. "You would look lovely in that shade of pink," she said to her niece.

Cécile looked at the yarn against the golden brown of her hand. The pink *would* look perfect, but...

"Monette Bruiller's mother has ordered a pink princess costume for her," Cécile said. "I want to be *une originale* for Mardi Gras—like no one else!"

Papa came in laughing from the hallway. "Cécile, you *are* une originale," he said. "You're my one and only daughter!" He shrugged off his heavy coat as their new maid, Ellen, a young Irish girl, stood waiting to hang it up. Then he crossed the cozy room to kiss Maman.

"Papa!" Cécile jumped up to give him a hug. "You're home early today," she said happily, following Papa across the thick carpet.

Papa sank into his chair. Cécile leaned against his arm and sneezed as a tiny puff of marble dust floated into her nose. Papa designed and carved beautiful things out of marble: statues that seemed almost alive, fancy urns and stately grave markers,

even fireplace mantels for homes and businesses. He spent long hours at his stone yard, and he was very successful.

marble urn

"We finished a job ahead of schedule, so I came home to enjoy my Cécé's chatter," he said fondly. "And just think, when Armand is back from Paris and we're working together, we'll finish early more often!"

Cécile was quiet for a moment. She missed Armand the most when everyone was together like this. "Armand will be a great stonemason, just like you, Papa," she said.

Cécile was quiet for a moment. She missed Armand the most when everyone was together like this.

"Just like you!" René shouted, running to wrap his fat little arms around Papa's legs. Papa patted René's black curls and looked across the room.

"How are you today, Octavia?" he asked gently.

Cécile looked up to see that her aunt had lowered her head over her work, unable to find her voice to answer Papa back. Cécile knew that Tante missed her husband terribly. Most days she was laughing, but sometimes she became very sad. This was one of those times.

At that moment, Cochon flapped his bright wings and squawked. Cécile suddenly thought of a way to cheer up her aunt. She tapped her father's arm excitedly.

"Oh, Papa, I know what my Mardi Gras costume will be," Cécile joked, clapping her hands. "I will be a bird!" she announced. "A great, noisy bird."

"A bird! A bird!" the big parrot squawked loudly. Laughing, Cécile ducked as he swooped across the room to land on her shoulder.

"A bird!" Maman took off her eyeglasses as she looked up from her knitting. "Cécile, you didn't say . . . a bird?"

"I think she did, Aurélia," Papa chuckled.

16

"Cécile, wouldn't you look charming wearing a parrot's beak to the ball!" said Tante Tay. She was smiling now.

"I'm a bird, too," René shouted. He pranced around Cécile with his arms spread like wings. Cécile flapped her hands and chased after him, squawking like Cochon.

"You really must stop playing that way, Cécile. Behave like a lady," Maman scolded gently, shaking her head.

Cécile captured her little cousin, who giggled and shrieked as she tickled him. Just then Grand-père peered into the noisy parlor.

"*Quelle horreur!* What a fright!" he boomed, pretending to be shocked. Ellen peeked into the parlor over his shoulder.

Cochon flew over to them and flapped rudely in Ellen's face. "Off with you, wild thing!" Ellen cried, batting him away with her apron. Then she bobbed in a curtsy to Maman. "Sorry, ma'am. I don't have much experience with birdhouses," she said solemnly, but the corners of her eyes crinkled with amusement.

"Grand-père," Cécile giggled, "welcome to our birdhouse!"

Maman sniffed, as a proper lady might in such a wild house. Then she winked at Cécile.

"Ellen," Maman said, smiling, "the birds would now like to have hot chocolate!"

Cécile burst out laughing at Maman's silliness. Oh, how she wished she could share this happy moment with Armand.

CHAPTER
TWO
—

FREE PEOPLE
OF COLOR

A few days later, as the sun poured through the tall parlor windows, Cécile's grandfather leaned forward from his chair. Lessons were over, the other grown-ups were out, and René was napping. Cécile had Grand-père all to herself, and she listened eagerly.

"Oh, that ship!" he said. "She rolled this way and that. I heard my captain call for all hands on deck. The wind howled and pulled our sails like an angry giant. Men ran everywhere, trying to take in the sails before the storm snapped our mainmast."

Cécile scooted her chair closer. "And then what, Grand-père? Were you running, too?"

Grand-père's eyes twinkled. "I was down below.

I thought: *I'm a carpenter's helper. I'm only a boy—what can I do?"*

"And?" Cécile urged him on.

"Before I knew it, I was scurrying up that mast."

"Like a spider!" Cécile squealed, squeezing her eyes shut to imagine a young boy in a raging storm, shinnying up the ship's mast as if it were a tree.

"Up and up, higher and higher," Grand-père chanted. "And then I tiptoed out on the yardarm and—*SPLASH.*" He slapped his hands hard onto his lap. Cécile gasped and her eyes flew wide open. Cochon sputtered on his stand in the corner and flapped his wings noisily.

"My *hammer* fell into the sea instead of me!" Grand-père laughed, his curly silver beard sparkling in the morning light. "No better way for a sailor to start his career, *non?"*

"Non! You were so brave," Cécile sighed with admiration.

"Oui, my Cécile. Because I loved the sea ... almost as much as I love you." He winked at her.

Cécile jumped up to plant a kiss on her grandfather's cheek. "Oh, Grand-père, when you tell a story, I can almost smell the sea. Armand can tell stories that way, too. I wish *I* could . . ." Her voice trailed away.

"When you've traveled to as many places as I have, chérie, it's easy. All the memories, the adventures, the stories—they are written right here." He tapped his chest.

Cécile hoped that wonderful stories would flow from her heart one day as well. "But I never have any adventures to tell about," she said.

"Don't worry," Grand-père replied. "Adventures you'll have, *ma chérie*. But you don't have to go around the world just yet to find them. You're my granddaughter, Cécile Amélie Rey—you'll find adventures everywhere, maybe right around the next corner. The important thing is to be ready for them." His voice dropped to a whisper. "Now, since your lessons are done, and your maman is not home yet . . ."

Suddenly Cécile knew what adventure Grand-père had in mind. "We'll go to the square for *pralines!*" She grinned. Sweets in the middle of the day! Somehow, when her grandfather was around, quite a few of Maman's rules were easily forgotten.

Grand-père took his big gold watch from his waistcoat and glanced at it. "Quick—let's leave before Aurélia comes back to remind us about dinner!"

"Oh yes!" Cécile clasped her grandfather's hand and pulled him up.

"Don't forget your hat, miss." Ellen popped into the hallway, holding Cécile's cloak and bonnet.

How did she know? Cécile wondered as Ellen firmly tugged the bonnet over Cécile's thick curls. Maman always said that a good servant knew just what was needed without being told.

"Ouch! Ellen, you're as bad as Mathilde. I can tie it myself," Cécile said, as Grand-père chuckled.

"And oh, don't go out in silk slippers," Ellen added. "You'll need boots for those awful sidewalks."

"The *banquettes* aren't so bad," Cécile protested, but she stepped into her leather boots, and Ellen swiftly buttoned them up. Finally, Cécile skipped out

porte cochere

beside her grandfather, through the porte cochere that led from their courtyard out to the busy street.

Ellen was right about the boots. The banquette was covered with a thin coating of mud, left over from a night of winter rain. Cécile didn't care. She was happy to be out with Grand-père.

Just ahead, she spied her tutor, Monsieur Lejeune,

turning the corner. He noticed them and waved. Cécile waved back, but then she quickly shoved her hand into her coat pocket. Her fingers were cold.

"No gloves again?" Grand-père clucked.

"Oh, Grand-père, I have so many *other* things to remember," Cécile said importantly.

"Such as?"

"Such as a new verse that I'm learning for Monsieur Lejeune."

"Shakespeare again?" Grand-père asked as they stopped to let a coal wagon pass. The noises of the square were getting louder. Horses clip-clopped past, pulling carriages. Somewhere nearby, a peddler sang about beads and trinkets for sale. Faint shouts of the men working on the boats drifted up from the levee.

"Yes," Cécile answered, raising her voice. "Listen:

> *Weary with toil, I haste me to my bed,*
> *The dear repose for limbs with travel tired;*
> *But then begins a journey in my head*
> *To work my mind, when body's work's expired...*

"Ah, it's about dreams." Grand-pére nodded. "Go on."

23

"Well..." Cécile hesitated. "That's as far as Monsieur Lejeune let me memorize. He says that I should work my mind with arithmetic instead of dreams. Can you imagine dreaming about numbers, Grand-père? That would be a *nightmare,* non?" Cécile giggled, and Grand-père laughed so hard that he had to pull out his handkerchief to blow his nose.

"Grand-père, look—there's Madame Zulime's candy shop. Her pralines are the best!" Cécile dragged Grand-père past the cathedral, not even stopping to listen to the bells strike the hour. As she threw open the shop's green door, she could almost taste the melted butter and roasted pecans.

Madame Zulime wore a crisp white apron around her waist. The colorful scarf she had knotted over her hair bobbed up and down when she moved her head.

"*Bonjour,* madame. Hello. Two bags of pralines, please," Grand-père said to the shopkeeper.

"Ah, Cécile! I see your grand-père is with you today. Perhaps he'll get you bonbons, too." Madame Zulime smiled at Grand-père and pointed to a tower of chocolates inside a display case.

Cécile headed right over to look. She heard the door open and close behind her.

"*Excusez-moi*," she heard Grand-père say.

"Watch where you're goin', boy!" came the rude reply.

Startled, Cécile turned. Two men had come into the shop. From their strange-sounding accents, she could tell they were outsiders—*Américains*, as French-speaking people in New Orleans called those who came from other parts of the country. One of the men glanced at Grand-père with a sour expression.

"Bonjour, *messieurs.* May I help you?" Madame Zulime asked.

"These French don't teach their slaves enough respect," the man said loudly to his friend. The friend tilted his chin in agreement.

Madame Zulime caught her breath.

Cécile's heart began beating very fast. Surely that man didn't think her grandfather, Simon Adolphe Rey, was anybody's slave?

Grand-père said nothing in answer. He stepped closer to the counter to take the package Madame Zulime had wrapped for him.

"Hey, you don't step in front of me!" The loud man moved as if he would shove Grand-père.

Cécile could feel her face flush rosy red. She'd never heard such nonsense. "How dare you, sir!" she burst out. "This is my grand-père, and we are *gens de couleur libres!*" Her voice shook a little, but she held her back straight and her chin high, the way she might if she were onstage.

The man stared at her with wide eyes when she spoke the French words, as if he didn't understand. He seemed confused for a moment, shifting his eyes from Cécile to her grandfather.

Grand-père put his hand on Cécile's shoulder. He was taller than the American, and so he looked down at him. "My granddaughter is telling you, monsieur, that she, like myself, is a free person of color. The Rey family is very well known and well thought of in New Orleans, sir. Be careful whom you insult here."

Madame Zulime quickly handed Grand-père a neatly tied bundle.

"*Merci,* madame." Grand-père took Cécile's hand. "Come, ma chérie. We'll eat a praline on the way home, non?"

Grand-père passed the Americans as if he didn't see them at all. Cécile followed him slowly and tried to do the same. When they were outside, she looked

"How dare you, sir!" Cécile burst out. *"This is my grand-père,
and we are* gens de couleur libres!"

back toward the shop, but a passing carriage hid it from sight.

"Grand-père," she asked, "why was that man so rude?"

Grand-père sighed. "Our city is changing. When I met your *grand-mère* here many years ago, New Orleans was French, African, and Spanish. In the years since, people have been moving to our city from all over the United States."

"*Les Américains*," Cécile said.

"Yes. And some of them think there are too many people of color here. Especially free people of color. They don't like it that we own businesses and homes and attend plays and concerts, just like everyone else. Colored people don't have so much freedom in other parts of our country."

Les Américains, Cécile thought. She'd never met any before, but if they were all as awful as that man, she didn't want to know them.

She bit into her praline and wondered why Madame Zulime's candy didn't taste as sweet as it used to.

A New Friend and Good News

Cécile was having the most beautiful daydream. It was opening night at a glittering theater, and she was the famous star of the show. The theater was full of people. She floated onto the stage, dressed in a fantastic costume. Golden ribbons were woven into her hair, matching her jeweled mask and shimmering gold dress. She bowed, and the crowd clapped wildly. She spoke her first lines. The crowd fell silent, captivated by her strong words and clear voice. Then she began to sing as sweetly as an angel—

"Oh! *Mais non*, Cécile! Did you practice at all?" cried her voice teacher, Mademoiselle Océane, tapping her baton on the arm of her chair.

Cécile had begun to sing off-key, and she knew it. Her final high note had sounded just like Cochon's screeching when she refused to share her praline with him. She wanted to squeeze her eyes shut so that she wouldn't see the unhappy face of her voice teacher. But then she remembered what Maman always said: "A strong person faces her mistakes."

"I'm sorry, Mademoiselle. I was—"

"I know, I know." Mademoiselle Océane shook her head. "You were only dreaming of your acting career."

Cécile felt her cheeks grow warm. "No . . . I mean, yes . . ." she sputtered.

Mademoiselle Océane's big blue-green eyes twinkled, and she laughed. Even her laugh tinkled like music. Cécile knew that Mademoiselle would understand. She was one of the best young opera singers in New Orleans.

"I know I can never sing as beautifully as you," Cécile began. "But maybe you could speak to Maman. Tell her I could study acting also!"

Mademoiselle Océane looked doubtful. "Cécile, I don't think—"

"I've already learned one of William Shakespeare's

30

poems completely by heart. They're called sonnets. Did you know? This one I learned just for you, Mademoiselle Océane." Cécile clasped her hands dramatically at her waist.

> *Music to hear, why hear'st thou music sadly?*
> *Sweets with sweets war not, joy delights in joy—*

"Ah! Music and sweets—my very favorite things," Mademoiselle interrupted. "*Très bien*, Cécile. Very good." She clapped her hands.

"I'm not finished," Cécile protested.

"You are here to train your voice, Cécile. I don't think your maman wishes you to have a life in the theater," Mademoiselle said kindly but firmly, tilting her head to one side.

Cécile shuffled the pages of her sheet music. Mademoiselle's look meant *Get back to work*. But Cécile's heart just wasn't in singing anymore. She sighed.

"Perhaps you should warm up again. Try a few notes," Mademoiselle Océane urged.

But Cécile had lost her focus. Even though she took a moment to look at her sheet music, the notes came out all wrong. "La-lah-li-LAHH!"

There was a noise outside the studio. Voices. *Laughing* voices. Cécile swallowed hard. Someone had heard her horrible performance. She hoped it wasn't Fanny Metoyer, who also took lessons. And Fanny had no talent at all!

Mademoiselle Océane stood and gave Cécile a hug. "Don't worry. Your mind is somewhere else today. Practice, oui? You'll do better next time."

Cécile nodded and whirled around, ready to face Fanny's not-so-nice remark. She ran and pulled the door open wide. "Why are you laughing?" she demanded.

But it wasn't Fanny who stood outside. Instead, there stood a girl just about her own age. She had light brown hair and wore a very plain dress. A handsome, well-dressed man stood beside the girl. He swung off his hat.

"Bonjour, mademoiselle," he said to Cécile in a serious voice. "I laughed because my niece looked so astonished when she heard the music coming from within this room. She was quite impressed!"

Cécile relaxed. "Really?" she asked, looking at the girl's curious expression.

32

The girl paused. "I've never heard anything like it," she said finally.

Knowing that her scales had been quite dreadful, Cécile readily accepted this strange compliment. She gave the girl a quick half-smile, and Mademoiselle Océane came to stand right next to her. Mademoiselle smiled warmly at the man.

He smiled back and took her hand for a moment. "Mademoiselle Océane, I would like to introduce my niece, Marie-Grace Rousseau Gardner," he said.

"Ah, your uncle has told me much about you," Mademoiselle said, reaching out to shake Marie-Grace's hand. "I am so pleased to meet you at last." Then she touched Cécile's shoulder. "Marie-Grace and Monsieur Rousseau, I'd like you to meet one of my favorite students, Cécile Rey."

Marie-Grace blushed and stepped closer to Cécile. "I'm pleased to meet you," she said softly, holding out her hand.

For a moment, Cécile only looked at her. The girl's accent sounded familiar . . . she was *une Américaine!* Would she be offended to stand in the same room with a person of color, as the man at the sweet shop had been?

Cécile wasn't sure how to behave. But she could almost hear her mother's voice in her ear saying, "A true lady *always* uses her best manners." Besides, when Cécile looked carefully into Marie-Grace's heart-shaped face, she felt that there was something interesting about her. So she set down her sheet music and shook hands. "Hello," she said with a smile.

"It must be wonderful to learn how to sing here," Marie-Grace said, sounding relieved.

"Oh, it *is* wonderful," Cécile replied, eager to start a conversation. "Mademoiselle Océane is the best teacher. She's very patient and understanding— even when I make mistakes!" She laughed, recalling her lesson, and continued. "My maman wants me to learn to sing well, and Mademoiselle makes me believe that I will someday. Does your maman want you to take lessons, too?"

Marie-Grace looked away. "No . . . my mother passed away when we first lived in New Orleans— when I was little."

Right away, Cécile gave Marie-Grace's arm a comforting squeeze. "I'm so sorry," she said, thinking of Tante Tay and René. "My uncle passed away not long ago. I know my little cousin misses him

Cécile set her sheet music down and shook hands with Marie-Grace.
"Hello," she said with a smile.

very much. René—that's my cousin—and my Aunt Octavia came back to live with us in New Orleans." As she spoke, another idea occurred to her. "So you were born here, too? But you sound like une Américaine."

Marie-Grace looked confused. "Yes, I *was* born in New Orleans. But I *am* American. Aren't you?"

"I'm from New Orleans!" Cécile insisted proudly.

"Isn't that the same thing?" Marie-Grace asked.

Cécile shook her head. "No, New Orleans is different from anywhere else in America. And people from New Orleans are different from people anywhere else, too! My grand-père says so, and he's been all around the world."

Marie-Grace smiled and nodded thoughtfully. "Compared to all the other places I've lived, New Orleans does seem like a different world."

Cécile raised her eyebrows. "You've traveled?" she asked. "Where have you been? I can't wait to travel and have adventures."

"Oh, we moved a lot, but I never had *adventures*," Marie-Grace said.

Cécile smiled. "Tell me about the places you've lived," she urged. Then she listened with interest as

Marie-Grace described Elton, Massachusetts, the tiny town she had lived in last.

It wasn't at all like New Orleans, Cécile thought, but still, the way Marie-Grace talked about it, she wouldn't mind visiting Elton. In turn, Cécile tried to make her own family and household come alive for Marie-Grace. She even flapped her arms, mimicking Cochon flying around the parlor.

"You *do* have adventures," Marie Grace said when Cécile stopped to catch her breath. "And you're lucky that you haven't had to move. Moving is hard."

Cécile was about to ask Marie-Grace exactly how many times she had moved when the door suddenly opened and Ellen poked her head into the room. Cécile couldn't believe that it was time to go home already.

"Sorry, miss. Am I too early?" Ellen asked, looking around the rather crowded studio.

With a start, Mademoiselle turned from Monsieur Rousseau and looked at the clock. It seemed that she'd lost track of time, too. "No, no," she said. "Cécile, until next time? And please do practice."

Ellen smiled. "Miss Cécile, get your cloak and be quick. The carriage is waiting." She began to gather Cécile's gloves and sheet music.

"Oui, Ellen." Cécile turned away from Marie-Grace to do as she was told, sensing excitement in Ellen's voice. Hurriedly she spoke to Marie-Grace over her shoulder. "Our maid is here to take me home. Perhaps we'll see each other again. I hope so. *Au revoir!* Good-bye!"

"Au revoir!" Marie-Grace answered.

Cécile grinned and waved as she rushed out the door behind Ellen, who seemed to be in an unusual hurry.

"What is it, Ellen?" Cécile tried to tie her cloak and keep up as Ellen walked briskly to the carriage. The young maid was usually so calm and collected that Cécile knew something must be going on.

"I've lots to do at home, that's all," Ellen said as the driver helped Cécile into her seat. But Cécile could see the twitch of a smile at Ellen's lips.

"Why? Is Maman expecting someone special?"

"You might say so," Ellen replied. "It's your brother! He just sent word that he'll be arriving from France in May—nearly three months early. Your mother is beside herself with happiness!"

Cécile caught her breath. Even though she was sitting, her knees felt wobbly. Armand was really coming home! She was thrilled—and yet suddenly she felt nervous at the same time. Her friend Monette's brothers had grown so tall in the past year. Armand had probably changed, too.

"It's a grand day, isn't it?" Ellen was saying.

Cécile was still deep in thought. First, she'd met a new and quite interesting girl. And now, to hear that her brother was returning so soon! A wide smile slowly began to spread across her face. Grand-père had said that adventures were right around the corner . . . and it seemed that he was right!

"Oh, Ellen," she exclaimed, "it's a *perfect* day."

MARDI GRAS SEASON

For the next few weeks, Cécile
felt like a spinning top. She saw
Mademoiselle Océane for voice
lessons and attended afternoon teas and Mardi Gras
parties with her friends. At home she had arithmetic
and geography lessons with Monsieur Lejeune,
endless fittings with the dressmaker, and needlework
with Maman.

One morning when Ellen was busy, Maman
asked Cécile to go along with Mathilde to the
market. Cécile was happy to leave her chores
behind and skip alongside Mathilde in the fresh
spring breeze. She loved the bustle and jumble of
the French Market, with its stalls of bright fruits

and vegetables and delicious-smelling pastries, its shouting merchants and crowds of chattering shoppers. She didn't even mind carrying a basketful of *baguettes*—long loaves of French bread—for Mathilde, because she knew there was a bag of pralines tucked into the basket, too.

Just as Cécile turned away from the bakery stall to follow Mathilde, she heard a familiar voice nearby making a very strange request: "Une banquette, *s'il vous plaît.*"

Cécile giggled and looked over her shoulder. There was Marie-Grace—and she was asking the baker for a sidewalk instead of a loaf of bread! Cécile hurried over to her.

"Marie-Grace, you really should work on your French," Cécile said. "It's baguette, not banquette!"

Marie-Grace blushed. "I'm not very good at French," she admitted slowly.

Cécile saw Marie-Grace's gaze drop to the ground. She realized that it wasn't very nice to remind Marie-Grace about her poor French.

Marie-Grace finished paying the baker and turned back to Cécile. "Maybe I'll learn more French soon, when I start school," she said, explaining that she'd been studying at home since she moved to New Orleans. "And my papa says I may be able to take lessons with Mademoiselle Océane, too."

"Oh, I hope so. Perhaps we'll see each other there," Cécile said. There were so many things she wanted to know about this Américaine. She looked around curiously. "Are you here with your cook?" she asked, wondering how many servants the Gardners had, and if they had a carriage and a driver. After all, Marie-Grace's father was a doctor.

Marie-Grace shook her head. "No, I'm here with Argos."

"Is Argos your maid?" Cécile asked. She'd never heard such an odd name before.

Suddenly a shaggy, dark gray animal ran up to her, wagging its tail and sniffing busily around her skirts. It was the biggest dog she'd ever seen. She hurriedly lifted up her basket and tried to step away.

"*This* is Argos," Marie-Grace explained.

"He's enormous! Does he bite?" Cécile asked with some alarm. But the dog was only nuzzling her hands gently. She relaxed.

"No! He likes you," Marie-Grace said.

"No—he smells my pralines," Cécile laughed.

42

"What are pralines?" Marie-Grace asked, giving her a puzzled look.

Cécile lowered her basket to search for the candy. She had gotten two wrapped for now and two for later. "They're my favorite sweet. Haven't you ever tried one?"

"I don't think so . . ."

"Here, have two," Cécile offered.

"Mmm," said Marie-Grace as soon as she took a bite. "My mother used to buy these for me when I was little! How could I have forgotten? Thank you!" Smiling, she wrapped the second praline and slipped it into her pocket. Argos trotted over to her side.

Cécile was pleased that Marie-Grace was so happy with her little gift. But now she was curious again.

"Are you really here with just Argos?" she asked. "I'm not ever allowed to go farther than our courtyard by myself."

Marie-Grace looked surprised. "I run lots of errands for Mrs. Curtis, our housekeeper. And for Papa, too. When we lived in Elton, I'd go to the pharmacy for him, and sometimes I'd do the shopping, just as I am today. Come with me to the next row so that I can get potatoes."

Cécile wanted to go with her, but she realized how long they'd been talking. "I'm sorry, I can't. Mathilde will be looking for me. But remember, this is the French Market. Ask for *pommes de terre*, not potatoes."

"Merci!" Marie-Grace waved and disappeared around a stack of wooden crates.

Cécile watched until Argos's furry body vanished too. For a moment, she didn't move. She was most impressed. Here was a girl who enjoyed being out in the world, doing things, just as she did. Marie-Grace didn't even know French very well, yet she had come to the market alone! This Américaine seemed shy, but she was certainly brave, too. She had spirit.

We're more alike than we are different, Cécile thought. And she was pleasantly surprised.

During the next few weeks, the girls saw each other as they came and went from Mademoiselle Océane's studio. After each lesson, Cécile delayed leaving so that she could talk to Marie-Grace or hear more stories about being a doctor's daughter in that

Northern place with the funny name.

One February morning, very near the time of the grandest Mardi Gras balls, Cécile sat on the floor in the middle of Maman's room, watching the dressmaker fit her mother and aunt for their ball gowns. Cécile was especially eager to get to her voice lesson today so that she could describe to Marie-Grace every detail of how Anna Day, the dressmaker, expertly snipped and tucked and stitched the silk to create the incredibly beautiful dresses.

However, even as Cécile counted the minutes ticking away on the mantel clock, Maman wouldn't allow her to waste time. Until she had to leave for her lesson, Cécile's task was to write the Armand Lists.

Ever since Maman had gotten the first word of Armand's new arrival date, the household had been in a buzz. Carpenters and painters were making Armand's bedroom bigger and brighter, and Grand-père was busily watching over their progress. Papa was making room in his shop so that Armand could join him at work. And Maman had begun to make lists of everything that Armand might possibly need or want when he returned.

"What might Armand want to eat on his first

day back at home?" Maman asked now.

Cécile knew the answer to that. She spoke the words aloud as she wrote: *Roast duck, oysters, shrimp and tomato bis... bisk...* "Maman? How do I spell bis—"

"Bisque? Oh yes! Your brother loves shrimp bisque. B-i-s-q-u-e."

Cécile looked up, frowning just a bit. After all, she loved the rich, creamy soup, too, yet she couldn't remember the last time Mathilde had made it for her.

"And don't forget the friends he'll want to see," Tante Octavia reminded her.

Cécile wrote *Pépé, François, Georges.*

"He'll need clothes," Maman said.

"Aurélia, the boy is coming from France. He'll have the latest fashions!" Tante Octavia stared at herself in the tall looking glass, wearing a dress with one sleeve. Anna Day grunted and shook her head as her quick brown fingers pinned the second sleeve perfectly into place.

"Boys don't care about clothes, Tante," Cécile exclaimed.

Maman nodded in agreement. "True, but our New Orleans weather is so different from that of Paris that he'll need new things. Let's begin with suits."

"What about handkerchiefs?" Cécile suggested. She'd been trying to think of a welcome gift for her brother. "I can stitch his name on a nice linen one! Can't I, Maman?"

"Of course, ma petite. Now, back to suits. One— no, I think two..."

Cécile bent close to the paper with a snort. *Two* new suits? Why, she was only getting one new dress for Mardi Gras. Her generous feelings about the handkerchief suddenly melted away. She loved Armand dearly, but everyone was making such a *fuss* over him. Suddenly, she was feeling quite grumpy about Armand.

Bong! Bong! The clock finally chimed. Cécile smiled up at its funny, curved wooden shape and lion feet.

"It's time for my voice lesson. Good-bye, Tante Tay! Au revoir, Maman!" she called as she made her getaway. She skipped down the stairs, eager for her lesson. At least Mademoiselle Océane always gave Cécile her full attention!

Ellen stood waiting at the bottom of the staircase with Cécile's hat, cloak, and music. As they left the house and walked out to the hired carriage, Ellen handed Cécile her gloves.

"What's he like, miss?" Ellen asked.

"Who?"

"Your brother, miss. I'm sure he must be a very clever young man to be studying in France."

"He's just a boy!" Cécile said sharply. She didn't mention that Armand had taught her how to draw, and play tag, and count in English and French. She didn't tell Ellen about the secrets they'd shared, like the time when she was five and Armand had pretended that he, and not Cécile, had spilled Maman's ink on the upstairs rug.

"Oh, I know," Ellen said quietly. "It's hard when they leave and hard when they return."

Cécile glanced up and saw that Ellen's eyes had a faraway look. "When my big brother Eamon went off to sea, I missed him something terrible, I did," Ellen said. "But when my ma turned the house upside down to welcome him home... I felt a bit put out, you know? Left out, I guess."

Cécile nodded slowly. "Armand is a good brother," she admitted to Ellen, and to herself, as the carriage eased to a stop.

"I'm sure he is, miss," Ellen said gently. "And here we are, then." She walked with Cécile from the carriage to the theater door, gave Cécile a smile, and turned briskly on her heel.

Cécile watched Ellen thoughtfully for a moment before hurrying upstairs to the music studio. Ellen had understood better than she had why she'd started to feel quite jealous about all the attention her brother was getting.

"Bonjour, Mademoiselle!" Cécile greeted her teacher cheerfully.

"Bonjour, Cécile," Mademoiselle Océane said. "Are you quite ready today?"

"Oui!" Cécile answered. She quickly arranged her sheet music on the stand near Mademoiselle's piano. Then she put everything else—including Armand and Mardi Gras—out of her mind.

The lesson went smoothly until the very last song. Cécile just couldn't hold the high note at the end.

"Try again," her teacher suggested patiently.

Cécile did. And again, and again.

Mademoiselle smiled sympathetically. "Your voice is tired. Perhaps we should try again next week, non?"

Cécile nodded gratefully and started to pick up her music. Just then, she heard hurried footsteps, and Marie-Grace threw open the door.

"Mademoiselle! Cécile! The most wonderful thing has happened." Marie-Grace pulled a heavy parchment square from her cloak and held it out for them to see. "Just wait till I tell you!"

Cécile knew at once what the paper was, but she didn't want to ruin the surprise Marie-Grace was about to share. She only smiled as Marie-Grace went on.

"Last night, a messenger brought this. It's an invitation to the Children's Opera Ball, and it's addressed to me!"

Cécile stepped forward, ready to burst out with congratulations and ideas for what Marie-Grace's costume might be.

"I'm so glad it arrived," Mademoiselle Océane said, beaming at Marie-Grace. Cécile's mouth dropped open. Mademoiselle wasn't surprised at all. She'd already known!

"You knew about it?" Marie-Grace asked, echoing Cécile's thoughts.

Mademoiselle Océane's eyes sparkled as she laughed. "Didn't I tell you? Never say never!" she said to Marie-Grace. "The Opera Ball is one of the best children's balls of the season, so you should have a wonderful time. I think I have a costume that will be perfect for you, too."

All at once, Cécile felt very cross. Everyone at home was full of Armand, and now, even her dear voice teacher was leaving her out. It was too much.

"Thank you so much," Marie-Grace was saying.

"I thought you might like a special treat," Mademoiselle Océane replied.

Cécile shuffled her music so roughly that she shook the stand. Why was Mademoiselle showing Marie-Grace such favor? They barely knew each other.

Mademoiselle Océane glanced over at Cécile. "Whatever is the matter?" she asked with concern.

Cécile couldn't hold her hurt feelings inside. "What about me, Mademoiselle?" she burst out. "Don't *I* get anything special? I've been your student longer!"

As soon as the words tumbled out, Cécile wished that she hadn't said them. Marie-Grace was staring at her. Mademoiselle Océane shook her head.

"Cécile, calm yourself," Mademoiselle said. "You and I have shared many special times, too. And you go to a lovely Mardi Gras ball every year, non?"

Cécile blushed hot with embarrassment. "Oui," she whispered to the floor, unable to look at Marie-Grace. Being upset herself was no reason to hurt a friend, she thought, studying the pattern in the rug. And she really was glad that Marie-Grace would have a chance to enjoy her first ball. She took a deep breath and raised her head.

"I'm sorry, Mademoiselle," she said. Blinking back tears, she faced Marie-Grace. "I was very rude just now. Please forgive me?"

"Yes, of course," Marie-Grace answered instantly. Her response was so kind that Cécile's mood quickly lifted.

"Your news *is* wonderful," Cécile said. She found that it felt much more pleasant to share in her friend's joy than to hold on to hard feelings. "Mardi Gras is truly magical," she added, smiling at Marie-Grace. "You'll see!"

Marie-Grace seemed relieved. "So you're coming to the Children's Opera Ball, too, Cécile?"

"Why, no." Cécile raised her eyebrows in surprise. "I *am* going to a ball," she said. "But we free people of color have our own separate Mardi Gras parties and balls."

Cécile thought she'd explained things quite clearly, but Marie-Grace looked more puzzled than she had before. "Why?" she asked.

Cécile shrugged. "Because . . . it's always been that way."

"Oh. I wish we could go to the same ball," Marie-Grace murmured.

Cécile realized Marie-Grace was disappointed that they wouldn't be able to attend her first ball together. A curious thought flashed into her mind. Why *had* things always been this way? Were the balls different? If so, *what* was different? Was it the music, or the decorations?

"Girls!" Mademoiselle was tapping the piano with her baton. "This year both balls will be held at the same place on the same evening. Perhaps you will see each other. Now, Cécile, shall we help Marie-Grace choose her costume? I have the fairy costumes that children wore in *The Magic Flute.* Marie-Grace, you may try them on behind the screen. I'm sure one will fit."

Mademoiselle Océane pointed toward a beautiful Chinese screen at the far end of the room. Peeking out from behind it was a pair of huge trunks,

overflowing with treasures. Cécile looked quickly at the clock, hoping with all her heart that Ellen would be late picking her up.

Soon, she was up to her elbows in gowns and masks and fairy wings. She chatted about some of her own favorite Mardi Gras memories while she helped Marie-Grace button and lace the shimmering dresses. They laughed at how one gown was much too big, the next uncomfortably tight. But finally Marie-Grace spun around, and Cécile gasped. This gown and the delicate, fluttery wings fit her perfectly.

"Oh!" Cécile clapped her hands. "It's *magnifique!*"

"It *is* magnificent—you look beautiful," agreed Mademoiselle Océane. Cécile watched as Marie-Grace put on the matching mask and twirled in front of the standing mirror in the corner, her eyes beaming.

"Thank you, Mademoiselle," Marie-Grace said. "And you too, Cécile. I never dreamed of such a beautiful costume."

Cécile grinned and scooped up an armful of sparkling gowns. Suddenly she was overwhelmed by a daring idea: On Mardi Gras, she could dress in a costume exactly like Marie-Grace's—and they could sneak into each other's ballrooms! It wouldn't be the same as going together, but still . . . they would have a Mardi Gras memory to share. And Cécile could see for herself just how the white children's ball was different from her own.

Mademoiselle Océane reminded Marie-Grace that she must change clothes to start her lesson.

"Go on," Cécile urged her friend. "I'll put the costumes away for you." Then she approached Mademoiselle Océane. "May I borrow a costume, too?" she asked quietly.

"Of course," Mademoiselle said with a smile.

Cécile took her time sorting the costumes by size, and when Marie-Grace was done dressing, Cécile slipped behind the screen. By the time she had chosen a costume and closed up the trunks, Mademoiselle was listening closely to Marie-Grace practicing her scales. Cécile gathered up her cloak, tossed it over the costume, and waved a cheerful good-bye.

When she met Ellen on the stairs, excitement was making her stomach quiver as if it were filled with dancing butterflies.

"Don't you look pleased with yourself," Ellen exclaimed. "You had a good lesson?"

Cécile nodded. She was *quite* pleased with herself and her Mardi Gras plans. She was about to have a great adventure right here in New Orleans, just as Grand-père had said.

CHAPTER
FIVE

DANCING FAIRIES

"Take a breath to calm yourself, chérie!" Tante Octavia said, and Cécile blew frost into the February air. The inside of the carriage was cold, but Cécile didn't care. She leaned across her aunt to look up at the dazzling light streaming from the windows of the Grand Théâtre, where the Children's Ball was being held.

The hired carriage eased to a stop. Cécile tugged at her velvet cape, being careful not to crush her wings. She smiled eagerly underneath her mask. Surely this Mardi Gras ball would be more exciting than any other!

"*Bonsoir.* Good evening, ladies." Two footmen

swung open the carriage doors and helped Cécile and Tante Octavia out. Each footman was dressed in white and gold; both wore pointy gold shoes and jaunty white hats topped with huge feathers that curled into the dark sky. They pointed the way up the wide steps. The faint strains of violins floated through the open doors.

"Isn't the music wonderful?" Tante Tay asked.

"Oh yes!" Cécile's heart began to dance before her feet could. She skipped up the steps. At the same time, dozens of other children were arriving along with their parents or chaperones. Some boys were dressed as soldiers. Some were clowns. She remembered the last ball that Armand had attended before he left home. He had been a handsome knight, wearing paper armor!

The crowd flowed into the theater, gently pushing Cécile and her aunt along. The lobby was a sea of colorful gowns and dark suits, and the air buzzed with chatter as parents and servants dropped children off. Cécile looked up at the high ceiling, painted with soft clouds and stars. Two candlelit chandeliers stretched their arms over the crowd.

The lobby opened to a sweeping marble staircase,

which led up to a landing and then branched off in two directions. Cécile saw that everyone followed the old custom: all the children of color were taking the stairs on the left side, while the white children  took the stairs on the right. Cécile wondered if Marie-Grace was entering her ballroom at this very moment with her father—or perhaps with Mademoiselle Océane. She inched along so that she could twist her neck to see upstairs. What was going on in the other ballroom? More than ever, she wanted to know.

"Here," Tante said just before they started up the staircase. "We'll check your cloak."

Cécile unfastened the hook at her neck and gently flipped her cape off her shoulders. She reached back to make sure that her wings were straight.

"My!" Tante Octavia said, helping Cécile with her cape. "What a beautiful fairy you are. That costume is enchanting."

Cécile felt a flutter of nerves. *What will Marie-Grace think when she sees my fairy costume? Will she go along with my plan?*

Cécile took a calming breath and looked around.

There was Agnès Metoyer. She had dropped her mask to look at Cécile's costume.

"A fairy! *Très belle*," Agnès said, offering a compliment.

"Merci!" Cécile blurted, giving herself away. Now that she had spoken, Agnès knew exactly who the fairy was.

"Cécile, is that you? Oh, I think I was mistaken— you've come dressed as a mosquito, haven't you," Agnès said haughtily.

Cécile wished that her fairy wand really was magic, so that she could make Agnès disappear. She dropped her mask to cast a disdainful look at Agnès's feathery green gown, ruffled blue gloves, and shiny blue slippers. She could hardly stifle a giggle. Agnès was Cochon, right down to his claws!

"And I didn't know you were coming as a parrot," Cécile said. "You're perfect!"

"*What?*" Agnès sputtered, looking down at herself and then up at Cécile in confusion. "I'm a flower!"

Cécile smiled. "But you remember my pet parrot, Cochon, don't you?" she began, before feeling Tante Octavia's hand on her elbow. She marched away, not even glancing back.

"Cécile! What would your mother say?" Tante whispered.

Cécile didn't feel a bit sorry, so she didn't answer. She followed Tante toward the marble steps and forgot about Agnès quickly. She ran her fingers along the smooth white rail, smiling all the time. Her father had cut the marble to build this staircase!

When they reached the second floor, the hallway was so beautiful that she wasn't sure which way to look. Paintings in ornate gold frames hung on the walls, and a thick red carpet cushioned the floor. Across from her, red-draped French doors led to a small balcony. Through a gap in the drapes, Cécile saw colorful fireworks dancing in the night. Music filled the air.

"This way, chérie." Tante Octavia motioned to the left.

Cécile gave a quick glance toward the other end of the hall, where closed doors hid the other ballroom. Her heart beat a little faster—would she see what was behind those doors before the night was over?

Then she turned to the left and followed her aunt down the carpeted hallway. In moments, she was inside a beautifully decorated ballroom. It glowed with soft candlelight from huge chandeliers and hummed with laughter and conversation. Peering across the gaily dressed crowd to the far side of the room, Cécile saw a lovely marble fireplace. That was Papa's work, too. Cécile had seen the drawings in his shop. The mantel was held up on each end by two fat marble columns, and its front had been carved in the design of a wide ribbon woven between baskets of grapes.

"Your papa's carving is beautiful, isn't it?" Tante Octavia said, giving her a hug.

Cécile couldn't answer. She was so proud that she wanted to shout. If only she'd thought to point out Papa's work to Agnès, instead of making her snippy Cochon joke.

"Do you see anyone you know?" Tante Octavia asked.

Cécile scanned the crowd. She nodded as she glimpsed a particular princess in an elegant pink costume. It was Monette!

"Good," Tante said. "I'll be off, then. Have fun!" She glided away.

The orchestra began a lively polka, led by the fiddles. Cécile couldn't keep still any longer.

"Monette!" she called with a wave.

"Cécile!" Monette's crown sparkled against her black curls as she pulled Cécile onto the dance floor. They were surrounded by girls and boys whom Cécile had known forever. Some had fathers who worked with Papa; some had mothers who took tea with Maman. Many of them had taken First Communion together at the cathedral. Everyone was laughing and happy. Even Fanny Metoyer gave her a half-smile from across the room.

Cécile sighed happily. When she became a famous actress, she would sail across the world— to France, England, perhaps even Russia—and after each stage performance, she'd dance all night at balls and parties just like this one . . .

After five dances in a row, Cécile began to have second thoughts about such a life. She left the dance floor to catch her breath and get some punch from the big crystal bowl on the refreshment table.

The musicians, who never seemed tired, began a different tune. This one was a couple's dance. Though she liked the group dances much better, Cécile lingered to watch girls and boys find their partners.

Armand had always picked her for the first
dance, and she missed him dearly for a moment. But
now that he had danced in Paris, would he feel too
grown-up to twirl with his sister? She looked down
at her cup, and the swirling reflections of the dancers
on the crystal made her think of the shimmering
wings of butterflies . . . or fairies . . .

Marie-Grace! This was a perfect time for the swap.

Cécile left her cup on the table and turned
quickly. No one seemed to notice as she stepped into
the great hall. It was almost empty. Two mothers
sat on a fluffy tufted bench and gossiped behind
their fancy masks. She walked slowly past them,
peering up at the paintings of roses and magnolias,
pretending that she was interested.

She passed the staircase and kept walking
toward the other ballroom at the far end of the hall.
She could see an arch, and beyond it groups of people
mingling and chatting. She heard music and kept
going. There—near the tall doors of the ballroom,
she spotted the glimmering curve of a fairy's wing.
She moved toward it, her heart pounding.

"Psst." Cécile tapped Marie-Grace on her
shoulder. When she spun around, Cécile almost

laughed out loud. She was looking at her twin!

No one noticed as one fairy hurriedly led the other along the hall to the balcony doors. Cécile pushed aside one of the heavy velvet curtains and turned the brass handle. The girls stepped out. The tiny curved balcony was only big enough for the two of them. Below were the shadowed gardens of the Grand Théâtre.

"Cécile, is that you?" Marie-Grace gasped.

Cécile lifted her mask. "Surprise!" She could hardly keep her voice down.

Marie-Grace looked at Cécile's smiling face with astonishment. When she looked at Cécile's costume, amazement crept over her face, and then she smiled, too. "Why, no one could tell us apart!" Marie-Grace whispered.

"I *know*—and I have a plan," Cécile said excitedly. "I want to see what the Children's Opera Ball is like, and you'll get to go to *two* Mardi Gras balls!"

Marie-Grace's eyes widened, so Cécile quickly went on to explain. "We'll both put on our masks; then you'll go to my ball at the other end of the hall, and I'll go to yours. After one dance, we'll meet back here. It will be easy. No one will ever guess who we are." She paused, expecting Marie-Grace to say "Yes!" right away.

Instead, Marie-Grace took off her mask and turned it nervously in her hands. "I wasn't invited to your ball," she said quietly.

"*I* am inviting you," Cécile said with confidence.

Marie-Grace seemed to consider the idea. "I don't know... You said that the balls for white people and people of color are always separate. Won't we get into trouble if we switch places?"

"*You* were the one who wished we could go to the same ball," Cécile pointed out. Still, she hesitated for a moment, remembering the unpleasant scene in Madame Zulime's sweet shop. What *would* happen if they were discovered? Cécile wasn't certain—but she was much too curious and excited to turn back now. "I want to find out what makes the Opera Ball so special. And we won't get into trouble because no one will ever know," she added. "It will be our secret!"

Cécile waited. In her heart, she felt sure that Marie-Grace—the girl who went to the French

Market alone—was bold enough to join in her plan. "Come on! It will be an adventure. *Our* adventure," Cécile said as her friend looked out over the courtyard.

Before Marie-Grace could answer, another crackle of fireworks threw bright colors across the sky and over the rooftops. Cécile sucked in her breath—the magic of Mardi Gras was everywhere.

"I'm ready!" Marie-Grace said, her face glowing pink—and yellow and blue—as a new round of fireworks exploded.

"Oh, I knew you were brave!" Cécile smiled happily.

Both girls put on their masks and briefly stood side by side, looking at each other as if they were gazing into a mirror. Then they slipped back into the hall.

"Remember, just one dance!" Cécile's fairy twin whispered.

Cécile nodded and waved. She watched Marie-Grace walk away, and then she turned to face the other ballroom. Her heart was thumping.

As she neared the arch again, she recognized one of Papa's customers, Mr. Perez, with his arm around his son. They walked right by Cécile. She zigged to the left. Was that girl looking at her? She zagged to the right.

With half a dozen more steps, Cécile was inside the ballroom. She stopped and scanned the room with great interest. The dancing girls and boys in their costumes and masks were mostly princesses and soldiers, just as at her own ball. The orchestra sounded the same, too. She peeked around the dancing children. Just as at her own ball, the orchestra musicians were all men of color, dressed in black with bright yellow silk waistcoats.

Maybe the food is different, Cécile thought. She scooted along the edge of the dance floor, brushing past mothers who gossiped behind their lace fans. She smiled to herself. Even the mothers were alike!

The long refreshment table was covered with a linen cloth. Punch was dipped out of crystal bowls into little crystal cups. Petit fours, tiny pastel-colored cakes, rose like a sugar mountain on a silver platter.

Cécile had barely reached for a cake and popped it into her mouth before her toes began to tap to the music. She watched the laughing, twirling dancers and stepped closer to join in. A girl swung out and caught Cécile's hand. Cécile gulped. She had forgotten that she was supposed to be Marie-Grace. What if this girl was a friend of hers? Thank goodness she'd remembered her gloves tonight.

"I told you not to dance!" another girl nearby burst out. She was wearing a shocking green gown that trailed behind her like a tail. It was an awful green—alligator green!

Cécile looked at her in surprise. Who was she, and how dare she order people around! Luckily, Cécile remembered not to speak this time. She simply laughed and spun herself back into the midst of the dancers. She lost sight of the alligator as she pranced and clapped. All the girls moved together in a swirl of colors, changing places with the boys. Cécile started to hum along with the music to keep from laughing out loud. What a good actress she was! No one suspected that she wasn't really Marie-Grace.

When the dance was over, Cécile rushed away. Behind her, the orchestra began a waltz. In the flickering candlelight of the hall, she walked slowly past some Americans speaking loudly about cotton prices, and then she ran.

Marie-Grace was already hiding on the balcony, waiting for her. "You were right, Cécile," she said happily. "It *was* an adventure. I had a better time at your ball than I did at mine. And I danced!"

"I danced, too!" Cécile said.

"Oh no." Marie-Grace's hand flew to her mouth.

Cécile nodded, hardly noticing her friend's reaction. "Yes, even though a bossy girl told me not to."

"What was she wearing?" Marie-Grace asked.

"Pooh." Cécile shrugged. "She looked like an alligator."

Marie-Grace caught her breath. "What did you do?"

"I just laughed and kept on dancing. You should have seen the look on her face." Cécile giggled.

Marie-Grace glanced anxiously over Cécile's shoulder. "We'd better go back to our own ballrooms," she said.

"Oui," Cécile agreed, still in high spirits over her success. "We can talk more at our lessons. Now we have our Mardi Gras secret to share!"

She suddenly gave Marie-Grace a quick hug, and her mask slipped down to her chin. Cécile caught it before it fell to the floor. As she slipped her mask back in place, a horrible thought struck her. What if her mask had come off while she was dancing?

"*Bonne nuit.* Good night," Cécile whispered, and then she flew away.

As she eased safely through the doors to her ballroom, she felt a little shaken. What if Marie-Grace's father, or her uncle, had called for Marie-Grace while the girls had changed places? What would Maman and Papa have said if Cécile Amélie Rey, a girl of color, had been discovered at the Opera Ball? Would her parents have gotten into trouble? Cécile's heart raced.

She looked up at a painting of three little dark-haired girls playing with a spotted puppy. Were they American? French? Gens de couleur libres? She couldn't tell. Just as no one had been able to tell her and Marie-Grace apart.

No one could tell.

Cécile's confidence slowly came back. She wandered toward the refreshment table, listening to the waltz that the orchestra had just begun to play. A waltz had been playing as she left the other ballroom, too.

She had imagined that the two balls might be different, when they were really so much alike. And she had wondered if the people in the ballrooms would be different, yet they seemed much the same, too. Yes, Cécile thought, somehow on this Mardi Gras night everyone seemed to be very much the same, no matter where they danced.

Everyone except her, of course. After this night, she was truly une originale—even if no one but Marie-Grace knew it!

SECRETS AND
PROMISES

It seemed that all of New Orleans was parading along the levee, dressed in finery. Cécile and Grand-père trailed behind the rest of the family. Cécile turned her face up to the May sun. Spring had always been her favorite season, because her birthday came along with the flowers.

Today her birthday was still a week away, yet she was almost trembling with excitement. The whole family had come down together to greet Armand's ship. After two endless years, her brother would soon be with them.

"Grand-père," Cécile asked, "do you think that Armand will still like gingersnaps for a snack and

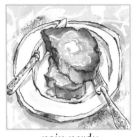

pain perdu

pain perdu for breakfast?"

Grand-père laughed. "I'm sure he will," he said.

But will he be the same loving, teasing big brother? she worried to herself. *And will he like my gift?*

Inside a small wrapped package, Cécile carried Armand's welcome-home gift. It was a linen handkerchief. She'd carefully sewn *AJCR* in blue on one corner of the white square. *Armand Jean-Claude Rey*. Maman had helped her get the design just right.

"Everything will be just fine," Grand-père said. Cécile glanced sideways at him, and he smiled. She smiled back and began to skip along. Grand-père, like Maman, was always right.

The levee road was wide and flat, with the busy city on one side and the even busier waterfront in the distance. Boats, barges, and ships of all sizes were grouped at the different piers that ran out toward the Mississippi River. The sweet smell from crates of Caribbean fruits mixed with the odors of horses and musty, wet wood. Cécile breathed deeply.

The family walked past mountains of cotton bales, standing ready to be moved. The slow, deep

songs of the stevedores who loaded
the bales rang through the canyons
of cotton.

stevedore

"Grand-père, what are they
singing?" Cécile asked. She almost
had to shout to hear her own voice.

"Work songs," Grand-père replied. "Sometimes
singing seems to make the work go faster. On the
plantations, the slaves sing. On the ships, we sailors
sang, too. The man with the best voice would start
off, and then the rest would join in."

Cécile and Grand-père stopped to listen. She
heard the deep calling of the leader: *"Way over the
water..."*

And then other voices, dozens of them, chanted
back in rhythm: *"Way over the water..."*

The leader sang on: *"When I go, remember me!"*

Swelling all around, voices sang back in perfect
harmony: *"When I go, remember me!"*

Cécile felt tingly all over. She thought about
the words. Probably some of the men were slaves.
Were they singing about the families they missed?
And how could so many men sing the same song so
beautifully without lessons or hours of practice? She

wondered if Mademoiselle Océane had ever heard
the stevedores sing.

Cécile's eyes wandered along with her thoughts.
The voices faded into the countless other shouts
and noises. Horses trotted past, pulling the heavy
drays that carried barrels to and from the crowded
barges. René shouted and waved back at Cécile from
his perch on Papa's shoulders. Tante Octavia leaned
close to her son, pointing out something on one of
the riverboats up ahead. Maman glided beside Papa,
half-hidden underneath her ruffled parasol. Cécile
could tell, without even seeing Maman's face, that she
was excited, too. Every few minutes, she gave the pale
yellow parasol a spin.

"Boat! Boat!" René cried, banging his little fists
against Papa's bare head. Papa only laughed.

Grand-père suddenly squeezed Cécile's fingers.

"Jean-Claude!" he called to Papa. "Jean-Claude!
Over there!" Grand-père was pointing to the giant
masts of a sailing ship docked a few yards away.

Cécile tugged his arm. "Is that it? Is that
Armand's ship? Oh, let's hurry, Grand-père!" Cécile
began to run.

"Cécile," she heard Maman whisper as she flew

by, because Maman never shouted. "Ladies don't run!"

Cécile ran anyway, glad that she was still a girl. She slipped between the fancy carriages lined up near the pier. Surrounding her were other families and friends, all shouting and trying to get a better look.

The front end of the ship, the bow, rose dark and slick from the water. It was taller than Cécile's house, and the mast seemed as tall as the cathedral spires. Cécile craned her neck to look up at the crowd gathering on the deck, ready to set their feet on land after the long voyage. No one looked familiar.

A narrow bridge had already been laid from the deck down to the pier. Cécile knew from Grand-père's stories that it was called the gangplank. Sailors in neat, dark uniforms came down first. They tightened the rope handrail and then stood at attention on either side of the plank.

The first passenger off the boat was a lady whose fantastic hat looked like a bouquet of silk flowers. Next were two Frenchmen so busy chatting that one of them almost lost his balance and fell. A sailor stood him upright, and he never stopped talking! Several older gentlemen came next. Cécile tapped her foot impatiently.

"Do you see him?" Maman touched Cécile's shoulder lightly. Cécile noticed that she was wearing the delicate lace gloves that Armand had sent for her birthday last year.

"Not yet." Cécile rose on her tiptoes to see better.

"Isn't that the top of his head?" she heard Papa ask eagerly.

"But our Armand has that touch of red in his hair, just like Cécile—" Grand-père said.

Cécile ducked underneath Grand-père's elbow and danced closer to the gangplank. She glimpsed a young man twisting his head to peer over the crowd. He had thick, dark hair like Maman. He suddenly turned. His eyes were the same hazel as her own. Cécile caught her breath. Could it be Armand? But this young man was so tall, and his shoulders were so broad. And he had hair over his mouth— a mustache!

Then his wide mouth broke into a grin. Cécile saw his dimples, and she knew for sure.

"Armand." His name came out as a whisper. She shook her head and threw her arms into the air. "ARMAND!" she yelled, but Maman didn't say anything about being ladylike this time.

78

"Where? Where *is* he?" Maman's voice rose, too.

"There's our boy!" Papa unwrapped René from his neck and handed him over to Tante Octavia. Then he dashed forward.

"Armand, *mon fils!* My son!"

And suddenly, Armand was right there, in the middle of his family. Maman grabbed one of his hands and Papa threw his arm across Armand's shoulders.

Cécile felt strangely shy, and she couldn't get her feet to move.

"Armand, I'll see that your bags are sent home." Grand-père clapped him on the back and headed toward one of the sailors.

"I have two crates also, Grand-père!" Armand called after him. His voice was deep, almost booming, like Grand-père's.

"Let's stop at the cathedral, Armand, to say a prayer of thanksgiving," Maman said. "Then we'll go home. Mathilde has outdone herself with dinner."

Even René hung from Tante's arms, chanting "AR-mand! AR-mand!" over and over.

Cécile wanted to say something—anything—but her throat was dry. She had never found it so hard to

79

speak in her life. Was this like stage fright?

"Cécé!" Armand freed himself from Maman and Papa. He bent toward her. "Don't you have a hug for me? Or must I pull your curls first?"

Cécile beamed up at him. The laughter in his eyes was the same. In an instant, Armand picked her up and swung her into the air. She threw her head back and laughed.

"Welcome home, Armand!" she shouted as her feet touched the ground. "Welcome home!" Cécile caught her brother's hand, and he held it tightly as they headed toward the square together.

A short time later, Cécile knelt in the cool quiet of the cathedral with her eyes closed. Armand knelt beside her.

Thank you for my family, she prayed. *Thank you for my brother.*

"Cécé," Armand whispered. She opened her eyes. In the dim light, she saw him quietly motioning toward the door.

What was he up to? Cécile glanced toward their

"Cécé!" Armand bent toward her. "Don't you have a hug for me?"

parents and aunt, who had knelt near the front of the church, closer to the altar. Then she silently followed Armand out of the pew, down the aisle, and outside.

"Maman won't be happy that we've left already," she said, but *she* was delighted. This was like old times with her mischievous big brother, when they used to share secret jokes with each other.

Armand pulled a lumpy package from his coat. "Here. It's an early birthday present for you," he said.

Cécile smiled broadly, but then her face fell.

Armand looked surprised. "What's wrong?"

"I have a gift for you, too . . . but I left it inside."

"Don't worry. We can get it later. Now, open!"

She didn't need to be told twice. She ripped open the wrapping paper and gasped.

There was the most beautiful china doll, with golden brown skin, brown porcelain curls highlighted by fine auburn lines, and hazel eyes.

"It's me!" Cécile cried. She flung herself around Armand's neck. "Thank you! Thank you!"

"I made the mold for her face myself," Armand told her proudly. "And a very kind French lady sewed the cloth body and made the dress. Do you really like her?"

"Oh yes! Your work is as good as Papa's," she said. "Together you'll be the best stone carvers in New Orleans!"

But Armand didn't answer. Cécile's smile faded as she looked at his serious expression.

"Cécé," he said finally, "can you keep a secret? A brother-to-sister secret?"

She held her doll close and nodded solemnly to her brother.

"Well... I've decided that I don't want to be a stonemason or a builder. I really want to be an artist—a painter."

Cécile swallowed hard. This was a truly important secret. Papa spoke so often of having Armand work side by side with him.

"But what will Papa say?" she asked.

"I don't know. I haven't figured out how to tell him. Just don't say anything, promise?"

"Oui." Cécile nodded.

Armand gave her a small smile. "Thank you, Cécé. You've become quite a young lady while I've been gone. I'll go and get your—I mean my—package." He darted back inside.

Cécile watched Armand disappear into the

shadowy cathedral, wondering what Papa would think about Armand's choice. Then she looked down at the gift her brother had given her. The doll's carefully painted face was beautiful. Cécile tried to think of a good name for her, but Armand's secret was clouding her thoughts. She stepped from the shade into the bright sunlight to see and think more clearly. The heavy cathedral door had barely clicked shut after Armand when she heard a familiar voice calling her name.

"Cécile! Cécile!" It was Marie-Grace, waving from the square. She came running toward the cathedral, with Argos loping ahead of her. Cécile stared in surprise and quickly pulled her skirt out of the way of his big, muddy paws.

"Cécile, I'm so glad I saw you," Marie-Grace said breathlessly before Cécile could get in a word. "I need your help."

Cécile's pleasure at seeing her friend turned to concern. "Marie-Grace, what's wrong?"

Marie-Grace hesitated. "Can—can you keep a secret?" she asked.

"Of course I can," Cécile said. But her stomach fluttered. The look on her friend's face told her that this might be another serious secret. "I promise that I will. What is it?"

"I found a—" Marie-Grace began. At that very moment, the cathedral doors opened wide, and Cécile's entire family spilled out, talking and laughing. Marie-Grace paused, looking uncertain.

"My brother's just returned from France," Cécile explained. "Come. I'll introduce you to my family."

"Oh no," Marie-Grace stammered. "I don't want to interrupt. Here!" She pressed a folded note into Cécile's palm, and with a swish, she and her dog were gone. Cécile was so stunned that she plopped down on the top step to read the note.

Can you meet me before lessons? It's important!

Cécile looked up to see Marie-Grace watching her from the square. Cécile nodded to her friend. Marie-Grace gave a quick wave and hurried off.

"What will she tell me when I see her next, *mon amie?*" Cécile whispered into her doll's ear. She traced the tiny nose and rosy lips with one finger. Of course, the doll didn't answer. She could keep secrets, too.

"Here!" Marie-Grace pressed a folded note into Cécile's hand.

Armand's shadow floated over his sister. "Look at this—it's perfect!" he said. She looked up to see him carefully tucking his new handkerchief into his jacket pocket. "*Merci beaucoup*, Cécé," he said, thanking her. Then he squinted at her. "Is everything all right?"

"Yes," Cécile answered, hoping that she sounded more sure than she felt.

"Well, come along then. Our feast awaits." Armand pulled her up gently and tucked her arm under his.

Cécile was still thinking. She had made promises that might be hard to keep. But Armand was her only brother, and Marie-Grace was different from any friend she'd ever had. Inside, Cécile felt concern for both of them, but she felt a deep, warm happiness at the same time. Both of them trusted her. She smiled to herself. Maybe Armand was right—she'd grown up. She somehow felt braver and stronger than she'd ever felt before. No matter what happened, she knew that she would keep their secrets. After all, she was Cécile Amélie Rey, and she was ready for anything!

LOOKING BACK

NEW ORLEANS
IN
1853

A street in the heart of New Orleans around 1850. To most visitors, the city looked and sounded more French than American.

In 1853, when Cécile's story takes place, Louisiana had been part of the United States for fifty years. Yet New Orleans, Louisiana's biggest city, was remarkably different from any other city in America. Visitors from other states noticed the differences immediately: the sound of French being spoken in streets and shops; the

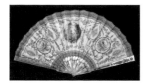
A lady's fancy fan

rich, deliciously seasoned foods; and the lively social scene, full of parties, balls, opera, theater, and horse races, even on Sundays.

One of the biggest differences was the way that people of different races and colors interacted. Unlike almost anywhere else in the United States, people of all colors lived in the same neighborhoods, shopped in the same stores, and attended the same theaters and churches.

There were many enslaved people in the city, just as there were throughout the South. But visitors were surprised to find that in New Orleans, many slaves could read and write, and some even ran their own businesses.

Visitors were even more startled by the city's thousands of free people of color, or *gens de couleur libres* in French. Many free people of color were well-educated and prosperous and had more luxuries than some white families had. Unlike Marie-Grace, well-to-do girls of color like Cécile were accompanied by a servant or family member whenever they went out in public and were raised to follow all the rules of

This fashionable young woman was one of the many free people of color who lived in New Orleans.

elegant society. Many well-to-do children of color were tutored privately or even sent abroad to study, as Cécile's brother, Armand, was. New Orleans' free people of color were not treated equally with whites, but they had more freedom and opportunity than black people anywhere else in the United States.

This painting from about 1845 reflects the close relationship between the young man of color, on the left, and a white relative.

Why were things so different in New Orleans? Unlike the eastern states, Louisiana had never been a British colony. Instead, it had been ruled by either France or Spain for nearly 100 years, and the laws of these countries were generally more tolerant of other races. Under French or Spanish rule, for example, slaves were allowed to earn money and buy their own freedom. Many families of color had both African and European heritage, and because of this, there was a wide range of skin colors among *gens de couleur libres*, from very dark to very fair.

By the early 1800s, one third of all the people in New Orleans were free people of color. Around this time, thousands more *gens de couleur libres* began arriving from the French colony of Saint-Domingue (now the nation of Haiti) after a slave rebellion broke out there. Many of these immigrants were educated

A scene from the Caribbean island of Saint-Domingue around 1800. Many French-speaking people from the island emigrated to New Orleans, and their traditions became part of the city's culture.

professionals and highly skilled craftsmen. Soon, New Orleans had one of the largest, most vibrant, and most prosperous communities of free black people in America.

But life started to get more difficult for them after Louisiana became part of the United States in 1803. People from other parts of the United States began arriving to govern and settle in Louisiana—but they did not understand or respect the way of life they found there. The American newcomers spoke English and were mostly Protestant, and they looked down on *all* Louisianians for their French language, Catholic religion, and unfamiliar lifestyle. In addition, many Americans were deeply prejudiced toward people of color, much like the men that Cécile meets in Madame Zulime's shop.

The American government passed harsh laws to limit the growth and rights of *gens de couleur libres*. For example, free blacks had to carry proof of their freedom at all times, and it became much harder for enslaved people to become

A New Orleans man named William Carrel carried this paper for years to prove that he was legally free.

93

free. Newspapers were forbidden to print criticisms of these new laws by people of color.

New Orleans changed in other ways, too. When Cécile was a girl, immigrants from Ireland, Germany, and other parts of Europe poured into New Orleans. Only a few worked in the homes of *gens de couleur libres,* as the Reys' Irish maid, Ellen, does, but the sheer number of new arrivals from Europe and other parts of America changed life for everyone.

By Cécile's time, for example, English had become the language commonly used in business, government, and schools. Families that once spoke only French, like Cécile's, now spoke both languages equally well. The city's original French-Spanish-African culture had become just one part of a bigger, more complicated mix.

Yet people of color remained a strong and important part of New Orleans life. They included some of the city's best-known builders and many of its ironworkers, carpenters, and bricklayers. The unique charm of New Orleans' older neighborhoods owes much to builders and craftsmen of color.

Men of color designed and built many of the "Creole cottage" style homes in New Orleans' older neighborhoods. These charming homes help give the city its distinctive look today.

(Right) Florville Foy, a free man of color, was known for the fine cemetery monuments he carved, such as this marble statue of a child with a drum.

(Left) New Orleans cemeteries feature thousands of above-ground marble tombs, because the soil is too wet for burials.

    Like Cécile's father, some of New Orleans' best marble-cutters and sculptors were free men of color, too. Florville Foy, for example, studied in France and established an extremely successful business carving marble tombs and cemetery sculptures. His work helped set the style for New Orleans' famous cemeteries, which now attract thousands of tourists every year.

    Other free men of color were respected musicians, writers, poets, artists, doctors, teachers, and business owners. Free women of color were noted as nurses, dressmakers, and sellers of produce and foods. Many women, like Cécile's mother, owned property.

    People of color flocked to opera houses, theaters, and balls, just as white people did. The two groups sat in separate sections of the theater and danced in different

Ladies and gentlemen arriving for an elegant evening at the French Opera House in New Orleans.

ballrooms, but the surroundings were equally luxurious.

One black man from Tennessee, James P. Thomas, first visited New Orleans as a slave in 1839. He returned many times as a free man in the 1840s and 1850s. Thomas wrote about the freedom and pleasure he found in New Orleans. There, he heard his first opera, enjoyed fine restaurants, walked freely anywhere in the city, and felt less prejudice than in any Northern city he had visited.

New Orleans' free people of color took pride in their unique identity. Public squares in certain neighborhoods—especially Congo Square in the Tremé neighborhood—became gathering places where people of color socialized and where musicians and dancers performed in the

*Wearing a turban or head wrap called a **tignon** (tee-yohn) was a stylish way to show pride in being a woman of color. The custom grew out of a time when women of color in Louisiana had been required to wear head scarves.*

traditional styles of Africa and the Caribbean.

The first collection of poems written entirely by African American poets was published in New Orleans when Cécile was a girl. A few years later, free people of color in New Orleans began to publish their own newspaper.

New Orleans' people of color also worked together to help the less fortunate members of their community, just as Cécile and her family help poor older people at La Maison. And although they could not vote, free people of color took an active part in politics, continuing to press for greater equality.

For much of the early nineteenth century, New Orleans stood out as a place where people of color enjoyed more freedoms than anywhere else in America.

Free girls of color in 1854

GLOSSARY OF FRENCH WORDS

Américains *(ah-may-ree-ken)*—Americans, or English-speaking people who moved to New Orleans from other parts of the United States

au revoir *(oh ruh-vwar)*—good-bye

baguette *(bah-get)*—a long, thin loaf of French bread

banquette *(bahn-ket)*—sidewalk. "A sidewalk" is *une banquette.*

bonjour *(bohn-zhoor)*—hello

bonne nuit *(bun nwee)*—good night

bonsoir *(bohn-swar)*—good evening

chérie *(shay-ree)*—dear, darling

de fête *(duh fet)*—festive, cheerful

excusez-moi *(ek-skew-zay mwah)*—excuse me

gens de couleur libres *(zhahn duh koo-luhr lee-bruh)*—free people of color

grand-mère *(grahn-mehr)*—grandmother, grandma

grand-père *(grahn-pehr)*—grandfather, grandpa

les Américains *(layz ah-may-ree-ken)*—the Americans

ma chérie *(mah shay-ree)*—my dear, my darling

ma petite *(mah puh-teet)*—my little one, my little girl

madame *(mah-dahm)*—Mrs., ma'am

mademoiselle *(mahd-mwah-zel)*—Miss, young lady

magnifique *(mah-nyee-feek)*—beautiful, magnificent

Mais non! *(meh nohn)*—But no!

maman *(mah-mahn)*—mother, mama

Mardi Gras *(mar-dee grah)*—a day of feasting and parties just before the somber religious period called Lent begins. "Mardi Gras season" refers to the several weeks of festivities leading up to Mardi Gras. The words *Mardi Gras* mean "fat Tuesday."

merci *(mehr-see)*—thank you

merci beaucoup *(mehr-see boh-koo)*—thank you very much

messieurs *(may-syuh)*—sirs

mon amie *(mohn ah-mee)*—my friend

mon fils *(mohn feess)*—my son

monsieur *(muh-syuh)*—Mister, sir

non *(nohn)*—no

oui *(wee)*—yes

pain perdu *(pen pehr-dew)*—French toast

pommes de terre *(pum duh tehr)*—potatoes

praline *(prah-leen)*—a rich, sweet treat made of pecans, brown sugar, and butter

Quelle horreur! *(kel or-ruhr)*—How awful! What a fright!

s'il vous plaît *(seel voo pleh)*—please

tante *(tahnt)*—aunt

très belle *(treh bel)*—very beautiful

très bien *(treh byen)*—very good, very nice

une Américaine *(ewn ah-may-ree-ken)*—an American woman
    or girl

une originale *(ewn oh-ree-zhee-nahl)*—an original, one of a kind

HOW TO PRONOUNCE FRENCH NAMES

Agnès Metoyer *(ah-nyess meh-twah-yay)*

Armand *(ar-mahn)*

Aurélia *(oh-ray-lyah)*

Cécé *(say-say)*

Cécile Amélie Rey *(say-seel ah-may-lee ray)*

Cochon *(koh-shohn)*

François *(frahn-swah)*

Georges *(zhorzh)*

Grand Théâtre *(grahn tay-ah-truh)*

Jean-Claude *(zhahn-klohd)*

La Maison *(lah meh-zohn)*

Lejeune *(luh-zhun)*

Luc Rousseau *(lewk roo-soh)*

Marie Conant *(mah-ree koh-nahn)*

Mathilde *(mah-tild)*

Monette Bruiller *(moh-net brew-yay)*

Océane *(oh-say-ahn)*

Octavia *(ohk-tah-vyah)*

Pépé *(pay-pay)*

René *(ruh-nay)*

Simon Adolphe *(see-mohn ah-dolf)*

Zulime *(zew-leem)*

GET THE WHOLE STORY

Two very different girls share a unique friendship and a remarkable story. Cécile's and Marie-Grace's books take turns describing the year that changes both their lives. Read all six!

Available at bookstores and at *americangirl.com*

BOOK 1: MEET MARIE-GRACE
When Marie-Grace arrives in New Orleans, she's not sure she fits in—until an unexpected invitation opens the door to friendship.

BOOK 2: MEET CÉCILE
Cécile plans a secret adventure at a glittering costume ball. But her daring plan won't work unless Marie-Grace is brave enough to take part, too!

BOOK 3: MARIE-GRACE AND THE ORPHANS
Marie-Grace discovers an abandoned baby. With Cécile's help, she finds a safe place for him. But when a fever threatens the city, she wonders if *anyone* will be safe.

BOOK 4: TROUBLES FOR CÉCILE
Yellow fever spreads through the city—and into Cécile's own home. Marie-Grace offers help, but it's up to Cécile to be strong when her family needs her most.

BOOK 5: MARIE-GRACE MAKES A DIFFERENCE
As the fever rages on, Marie-Grace and Cécile volunteer at a crowded orphanage. Then Marie-Grace discovers that it's not just the orphans who need help.

BOOK 6: CÉCILE'S GIFT
The epidemic is over, but it has changed Cécile—and New Orleans—forever. With Marie-Grace's encouragement, Cécile steps onstage to help her beloved city recover.

A SNEAK PEEK AT
THE NEXT BOOK IN THE SERIES

Marie-Grace

AND THE ORPHANS

 As Marie-Grace Gardner copied out her French lesson, light from the oil lamp glimmered off the glass medicine bottles in her father's office. The room was quiet. Even though it was late, her father, Dr. Thaddeus Gardner, was still out seeing patients.

Marie-Grace could hardly wait for Papa to return so that she could tell him her good news. A girl named Isabelle had joined her class today. Marie-Grace was usually shy. But she knew how hard it was to be the new girl in school, so she had worked up her courage and talked to Isabelle. The two of them had sat together at lunch, and Marie-Grace had been delighted to discover that Isabelle was quite friendly.

So far, Marie-Grace's only true friend in New Orleans was Cécile Rey. But Cécile and Marie-Grace did not go to school together. They usually saw each other only on Saturdays, when they both took singing lessons at the Royal Music Hall. *It would be nice to have a friend at school*, thought Marie-Grace, smiling.

As Marie-Grace dipped her pen in the inkwell,

she remembered that she had bad news to share with her father, too. Their new maid, Annie, had argued with their housekeeper, Mrs. Curtis. Annie had announced that she was quitting, and Mrs. Curtis had gone to bed early with a headache.

Now Marie-Grace was the only one in the household who was awake. As she struggled with her French verbs, she listened for the sound of her father's key in the lock. But besides the scratching of her steel pen on the paper, all Marie-Grace could hear was the clock ticking and rain gently tapping on the front window.

Suddenly, a loud knock broke the silence. Marie-Grace was so startled that her hand jumped, leaving a heart-shaped ink spill on the page. Her dog, Argos, raced to the door, barking.

Marie-Grace knew that she should not unlock the door at night. If anyone came to the office after dark, Mrs. Curtis was supposed to answer the door. But Mrs. Curtis was asleep, so Marie-Grace blotted the ink stain and hoped that whoever was at the door would go away.

Then another knock sounded, even louder than the first. Marie-Grace guessed that the visitor could see the lamplight and thought that Dr. Gardner was in his office. "The office is closed," she called above Argos's barking. Then she repeated in French, *"Le bureau est fermé."*

A woman's muffled voice made a short reply. It sounded like, "Please take . . ." Marie-Grace could not understand the last few words.

After a few moments, Argos stopped barking, but he stood at the door, whimpering. Marie-Grace went to the front window and peeked around the curtains. The streetlamp on the corner cast a dim light, and Marie-Grace could see that the woman had gone away, but she had left a basket on the step.

That must be what Argos is excited about, Marie-Grace realized. Her father often took care of people who had no money, and sometimes they left food as payment. One farmer had delivered a large smoked ham.

Argos whined impatiently. "All right," Marie-Grace whispered. "We'll see what it is."

She opened the door. A light rain was falling, and the air smelled like the muddy levees along the Mississippi River. Holding tight to Argos's collar, Marie-Grace leaned down to look at the basket. There was a lump of something inside, but it was covered by a cloth. Curious, Marie-Grace pushed aside the cloth. Then she gasped. She let go of Argos's collar and picked up the basket. She carefully lifted the cloth and looked again. There could be no mistake—a sleeping baby lay nestled inside the basket.

"Gracious sakes!" breathed Marie-Grace as she stared at the child. She looked up and down the street. At first, she didn't see anyone. Then she caught a glimpse of movement at the end of the block. A slender woman with a cloth tied around her head was standing half-hidden by a building. *"Madame!"* Marie-Grace called. "Is this your baby?"

Instead of answering, the woman disappeared around the corner. A fresh breeze blew down the street, bringing with it a sprinkling of rain. The baby shuddered and gave a soft cry in its sleep. Argos looked up at Marie-Grace questioningly.

Marie-Grace knew what she had to do. She carried the basket into her father's office and carefully set it on the desk. By the light of the oil lamp, she saw that damp ringlets of hair framed the baby's face. The child held its tiny fist to its

There could be no mistake—a sleeping baby lay nestled inside the basket.

mouth, and its eyes were scrunched closed. "Hello!" she whispered to the sleeping infant. "You didn't get rained on, did you?"

The baby was wearing a patched gown that looked as if it had been made from an old flour sack. Marie-Grace touched the cloth and the baby woke. The child's blue-gray eyes looked up at her anxiously, a thin line forming between its delicately arched eyebrows.

"Don't cry," Marie-Grace said, gently stroking the baby's cheek. As she leaned over the basket, she sniffed something that smelled like coconut. "You'll be all right now. My papa will be home soon, and—"

A stern voice interrupted her. "Marie-Grace, why is the door open?" It was her father. She had not even heard him come into the office. As he took off his overcoat and hat, he began to lecture her. "I've told you a thousand times that you must keep the office locked when you're alone here at night."

"A woman knocked on the door, Papa," Marie-Grace explained. "She went away, but look what she left." Marie-Grace stepped aside so that her father could see the basket.

"Who's this?" he asked, his voice softening.